P9-CDW-666

Discover the wonderful world of Pooh in these eighteen heartwarming stories from the Hundred-Acre Wood. By collecting each book, children will learn about how things grow, where honey comes from, and other fun facts about nature, while at the same time discovering what friendship is all about. In every delightful adventure, Pooh and his steadfast pals demonstrate that sharing, cooperation, tolerating differences, teamwork, helpfulness, a positive outlook, flexibility, determination, and honesty make a happier world for everyone. Come "out & about" with Pooh, and share the fun with your child!

**W**atch your child grow and learn with each new addition to this special Pooh library!

Published by Advance Publishers
©1996 Disney Enterprises, Inc.
Based on the Pooh stories by A. A. Milne © The Pooh Properties Trust.
All rights reserved. Printed in the United States.
No part of this book may be reproduced or copied in any form
without written permission from the copyright owner.

Written by Helene Chirinian
Illustrated by Arkadia Illustration Ltd.
Designed and Illustrated by Vickey Bolling
Produced by Bumpy Slide Books

ISBN: 1-885222-73-4
10 9 8 7 6 5 4 3

# Pooh
## Parents' Guide

# Disney's Out & About With Pooh
### A Grow and Learn Library

# Disney's Out & About With POOH...and YOU!

Introducing your child to the wonderful books in Disney's Out & About With Pooh series will inspire a desire to read that lasts a lifetime. Good reading habits are a crucial part of a child's success — at school and beyond — because they are the foundation for processing information. As your child begins preschool or elementary school, reading at home and developing language skills will give him or her an extra boost.

Schools stress two areas of reading — the act of deciphering letters and putting them together in words that make sense, and the understanding of what is read. But most schools don't stop there. They emphasize "whole language," encompassing reading, understanding, writing, and spelling as a natural, integrated process.

Children learn to read using *phonics*, a teaching method that encourages them to "sound it out" and put consonants and vowels together to read words, and *sight reading*, in which word recognition is almost instantaneous. Most children learn through a combination of both. How and when they learn depends upon their development and exposure to reading and oral language. As children learn to read they will develop comprehension, understanding not only the words, but the ideas and sequence of language.

Here are some general guidelines to help your child love reading and language:

- Children who see their parents and siblings read think of reading as a natural activity for their family, so make sure your child sees that you enjoy a variety of reading material.
- When your child asks questions, answer them as fully as possible. If there are questions you don't know the answers to (Why are frogs green?), admit it, and demonstrate how you can find out together by going to the library or by using references you might have at home.
- Take your child to get a library card. In most cities, children can get them as soon as they can write their names.
- Ask children questions about their play and their day, and listen attentively as they relate events to you. Gently correct mispronunciations

or grammatical errors occasionally. If you model good grammar and vocabulary, children will pick it up.

- Read a bedtime (or anytime!) story. This is a time-honored way for parents and children to bond and to share reading. As you read, show children how you proceed from left to right, starting at the top and ending at the bottom of the page. Show children how to turn pages, how illustrations relate to the story, and how to respect and treat books. Read to them every day if possible. Too tired? Ask your child to tell *you* a story! Soon he or she will want to "read" from favorite books. It may begin with imaginative retellings but will soon progress to real reading!

## How to Use This Guide

This guide contains lively ideas to get the most out of this series with your child. Start by reading the brief summary of the book. Then discover how to build important language and thinking skills. Continue by having fun with activities that will make each book memorable for you and your child. Each activity in this series has an educational basis, was written by educators and tested by children.

## Getting Started

Familiarize children with the alphabet by teaching them the alphabet song, drawing and cutting out letters, and helping them write their names and the names of everyone in their family. Provide children with crayons, paper, pencils, and marking pens so they may begin to write and draw their own thoughts, stories, and experiences. Keep these supplies in a special place so little artists and writers will have easy access to them. Stress that drawing and writing are for paper, not walls. Respect the child's supplies and ownership of them.

Children often ask about the meaning of words they see in ads, on TV, and even in junk mail. This is a great opportunity to point out beginning and ending word sounds and to practice sight recognition.

As you read each book with your child, he or she may want to go back and read it time and time again. This may become tiresome for you, but children are building relationships with books, characters, and language. Favorite books may very well accompany them to college and become cherished by future generations — thanks to you, your child's first teacher. So enjoy this series and make it your own, for the sake of you and your child!

# Good as Gold

As the merry group headed home, Owl cleared his throat. "Did I ever tell you what my Uncle Midas said about good friends?" he asked.

"No, what?" wondered Pooh.

"They're as good as gold!" replied Owl.

And Pooh and his friends had to admit they were feeling very rich indeed.

**W**hile searching for his missing honey pot, Pooh and his friends see a beautiful rainbow. Owl tells them that there's supposed to be a pot of gold at the end, so they all set out in search of the treasure. Instead, the friends stumble upon other precious finds: a rock, a robin's egg, and a nest. The gold eludes them, but Pooh saves the day when he finds his missing honey pot and fills it with berries in the colors of the rainbow. As the group heads home after a fun-filled day, they all agree that they are very rich indeed. This story teaches children that:

- it's fun to explore with friends.
- friendship is precious.
- nature is filled with treasures.
- gold is a precious metal.
- rainbows have no beginning or end.

## What's It All About?

Help your child understand what is read by asking him to list what Pooh and his friends found, in order. This will encourage him to mentally sequence events as he reads.

Then try these comprehension questions:
- How many honey pots was Pooh supposed to have?
- What did Owl's uncle say about rainbows?
- What color was the robin's egg?
- Where did Pooh leave his third honey pot?

## Thinking Time

Gold is valuable, but your child might not know why. Talk about valuable things, including those that aren't material goods, to give your child the opportunity to think about what is valuable in the world and in his life. Then ask these questions:

- Which would you rather have, gold or honey? Why?
- Why were the friends willing to share the gold they might find?
- Why do you think rainbows disappear?
- Would you share a treasure with a friend? Why or why not?

## Treasure Hunt

Go outside for a treasure hunt. Tell your child to keep looking down or up for treasures. If he isn't sure what a treasure is, begin by picking up a pretty or interesting leaf, rock, or even weed. Collect the treasures in a box. When you have ten or so, dump them out and discuss what is precious about each one. For example: "This is a leaf. It's like no other leaf in the whole world." Or "This is a rock. It's smooth and shiny and would look nice in the garden."

## Let's Write

Write a story about your treasure hunt, then illustrate it with your child. Use ordinal numbers to emphasize sequence. For example: "First, we went to the park. Second, we found a big, green leaf. Third, we found a smooth, shiny rock." Make sure you write the story in large letters, using both upper and lower case to model sentence writing. If your child wants to copy yours on his own piece of paper, that's

great. If it doesn't look exactly the same, don't be concerned. Your child's desire to write is what's important.

## Rock Painting

Gather some rocks, the smoother the better. Discuss with your child what kind of animal or person the rock should be, then paint it with large brushes and poster paints (liquid tempera). With smaller brushes, add facial and other features. Let your treasure dry and display it proudly.

## The Rainbow Room

Using many colors of construction paper cut and taped together, help your child make a giant rainbow. Place it over his bed so that when he's tucked in at night, the treasure that is found at the end is something much more valuable than gold — his own precious self!

# A Perfect Little Piglet

"Hmmm," Piglet thought. "Bees are small. Snowflakes are small. Hummingbirds and their nests are small. Maybe being small isn't so bad, after all. Of course, I still can't reach Pooh's teacups."

And, feeling just a bit better, he began to whistle and skip through the woods.

**P**iglet is distressed to find that he can't reach the teacups in Pooh's cupboard, and decides that being small is definitely a disadvantage. But as he bumps into each of his friends, helping some, learning from others, he discovers that many wonderful things in the world are indeed small, and he comes to realize that he is perfect just the way he is. Piglet's story will teach children that:

🐾 friends can help you feel good about yourself.

🐾 everyone is unique and has something valuable to contribute to society.

🐾 they have the ability to solve problems.

🐾 tiny things inhabit and enrich our world.

## What's It All About?

Simple questions help your child acquire essential reading comprehension skills. As you read the story a second time, asking such questions as "What color is Tigger?" and "Who has a tail?" will enable children to relax and feel that questions are fun. Later you may proceed to more complex questions, but setting a relaxed mood for comprehension feedback is most important. Try questions such as these:

• Why does Piglet go to Pooh's house?
• What happened to Piglet's hat?
• What does Eeyore always lose?
• What were the small things that Piglet discovered?
• What does Piglet do with the nest?

## Thinking Time

Get children imagining with these thought-provoking questions:

- Why does Piglet feel sad when he can't reach the teacups?
- How do you think snowflakes would feel on your tongue?
- What would happen to the snowflakes in your mouth? Why?
- Why is it wonderful to be small?

## Snowflakes That Last

After you've talked about what happens to snowflakes and why, make paper snowflakes. Blunt scissors, white paper (as light as possible; heavy paper is hard to cut for tiny fingers), and several folds and cuts will make beautiful designs to attach to windows, walls, or the refrigerator. Experiment together — remember, no two snowflakes are exactly alike! Try colored tissue or other paper for variety and brightness. Make sure the paper and cuts are large, so young children will have fun and feel successful.

## Baby Animals

Discuss the title of this book, *A Perfect Little Piglet*. What is a piglet? Give your child a chance to ponder and respond, then bring up this intriguing question: If a baby pig is a piglet, then what is a baby cat? She will probably know the answer to that one, so go on! Talk about what baby dogs, sheep, geese, chickens, ducks, and cows are called. Let your child think of some other animals. Look up the names for their babies in a dictionary if you don't know the answers. Or have fun with language and make up your own "baby" words. Could a baby dinosaur be a dinolet? If a cat is a kitten, is a mouse a mitten? This activity can be followed up with drawings of adult animals and their families, or animal bingo, or concentration. Make your own game with pictures drawn by you or your child, or coloring book or magazine pictures.

## Feeding the Birds

Talk about the bird's nest in the story. Tell your child that birds need help to find food, too. Make a bird feeder out of a two-liter plastic soda bottle. Cut out the center of the bottle (see illustration) before you have your child get started. Paint leaves, birds, trees, or whatever designs your child wishes on the bottle with puffy paint. Attach a string to the top and put some wild bird seed in the bottom of the bottle. Tie the bird feeder to a tree branch, overhang, or any other place where you've seen birds. Make sure it's a place where birds can perch, because there's nothing to hold onto on the feeder. Birds will flock to the feeder, and your child will feel as good as Piglet did when he rescued the little nest.

# The Friendship Garden

"Well, Pooh, how do you like your garden now?" asked Rabbit.

"It's *our* garden," said Pooh. "Because without all of you, I wouldn't have a garden at all!"

Pooh, Piglet, Roo, and Rabbit each dug up a sunflower. They carefully carried the flowers back to Pooh's garden and planted them there.

**P**ooh, a well-known bear of little brain, admires Rabbit's sunflowers and decides to plant some of his own. But in spite of Piglet's and Roo's help, the seeds somehow end up in Pooh's honey pot instead of in the ground. Pooh's friends save the day, and lovable Pooh ends up with big yellow flowers that are smart enough to turn themselves toward the sun. Pooh's story will teach children:

- about friendship and acceptance of others, even though they may have faults.
- how working together builds friendship and good times.
- how to plant a garden.
- about cooperation and nonjudgmental behavior.

## What's It All About?

Build reading comprehension slowly as you ask your child questions about the story. Make sure the questions are integrated into the reading experience so the child will not feel threatened or "on the hot seat." Here are some sample questions to ask, but tailor the questions to your child's interest and attention span.

- Why didn't Pooh have any honey left?
- Why did Pooh think the sunflowers were so smart?
- How did Pooh's friends help him with his garden?
- What did Pooh do with the seeds?
- How did the sunflowers get into Pooh's garden?

## Thinking Time

Critical thinking skills are important stepping-stones in a child's development. These skills go beyond recalling information; they help children find logical solutions to problems and process the information provided to them. Try some "thinking" questions like the ones below. Make up your own, too.

- Why do you think bears like honey so much?
- Why did Pooh's friends want to help him with his garden?
- Why did Pooh call his garden *The Friendship Garden*?

## Rhyme Time

Pooh makes up a clever rhyming song. You and your child can add to it or make up your own, for example:

> Read a book,
> Take a look.

Keep the rhymes simple. For practice, recite a Mother Goose rhyme together. Talk about rhyming words. Use rhymes in everyday conversation, such as:

> Mommy said,
> Make your bed.

## Pooh Play

Children love to dramatize anything! Help your child act out a scene from the story. Get out some small garden tools and pretend to plant a garden. Talk about how hard you are working and what you're planting. Act out a scene between Pooh and his friends. Make backdrops using butcher paper, old brown wrapping paper, or even newspaper. Then draw and color Pooh's house or other scenery for playacting.

## How Does Your Garden Grow?

Help your child plant a real garden. Buy seeds that will germinate quickly and plant them in the dirt, or sprout birdseed or other seeds in a saucer with a touch of water, or buy started plants of vegetables or flowers for more certain success. Children love to watch gardens grow, especially if something edible results!

## Pooh Puzzle

Doing puzzles helps children enhance visual perception skills. Have your child draw and color a picture of Pooh and his friends, then glue the picture to a piece of cardboard for him. Cut the cardboard-backed picture into seven or eight puzzle pieces. Mix them up and give them to your child to put together.

## Try Some Phonics

Choose some words on a page that begin with the same consonant. Read them aloud, emphasizing the beginning sound. Ask your child what is the same about the words. For example: Pooh, Piglet, paw, plant.

# Look Before You Bounce

As Pooh finished his song, someone came bouncing along who was even faster than he was. It was Tigger, and he didn't seem to notice the turtle in his path. Pooh waved for him to stop, but Tigger still wasn't paying attention. Tigger bounced into the turtle, and the two of them went sprawling across the ground.

**E**nergetic Tigger disturbs his friends, not to mention the plants and creatures of the Hundred-Acre Wood, as he recklessly bounces about the landscape without a care in the world. But when he lands on a prickly thistle and hurts himself, a wiser, more careful Tigger decides to take his friends' advice to look before he bounces. This story helps children understand that:

- you should take the comfort and feelings of others into consideration.
- plants and animals protect themselves in different ways.
- you can be careful and have fun at the same time.
- you can learn from experience.

## What's It All About?

After reading the book for the first time, have fun with reading comprehension by establishing signals to show when certain events in the story occur. For example, bounce when you think Tigger will bounce, or hold your nose when the skunk appears.

Also try these questions:
- How does Tigger's twitch turn into a bounce?
- What happened to Rabbit's carrot pile?
- What did the turtle do when Tigger bounced into him?
- What might a skunk do when frightened?

## Thinking Time

Tigger's friends urge him to be more careful by looking before he bounces. Discuss with your child other ways of being careful — taking your hand and looking before crossing the street, for example. Talk about how being careful keeps your child and others safe. Then try these questions:

- Why do you think Tigger likes to bounce?
- Why didn't Tigger pay attention to where he was going?
- How does a shell keep a turtle safe?
- Why did Tigger decide to look before he bounced?

## Sorting It Out

Rabbit sorted his carrots according to size. Have your child do the same with carrots, strawberries, or any fruits or vegetables that vary in size. The reward for good sorting can be eating them as is or helping a parent make a delicious dish using the fruit or vegetable. Sauteed carrot "coins" or strawberry shortcake with whipped cream are always appreciated!

## Safe and Sound

How do animals keep themselves safe? They use claws, teeth, a hard shell, sharp quills, or even smells for defense. Discuss which animals use which, then review the rules you have with your child about keeping herself safe. For example: Don't talk to strangers; don't open the door unless Mommy or Daddy tells you to; don't play with matches. Make an "I Know How to Be Safe" chart that you write and your child illustrates. Post it in a conspicuous place and refer to it often, adding helpful hints when situations arise.

## Getting to Know You

Piglet, a friendly fellow, was trying to make friends with a skunk when Tigger bounced by. Ask your child how she makes a new friend. This is an important skill for your child to develop. Talk about her friends and why she likes them. Then talk about the best ways to make new friends.

## Role-Playing with Tigger

Have your child play the role of Tigger while you play the turtle or another animal that Tigger disturbed. Create dialogue as you go along. This exercise is fun and will teach your child to be sensitive to others and to be able to think on her feet. Help her along if she gets stuck for words.

For example:
Turtle: Hey! You knocked me over.
Tigger: I was bouncin'!
Turtle: You almost hurt me.
Tigger: I didn't mean to.
Turtle: You didn't say that you're sorry.
Tigger: I am, and I'll be more
      careful next time, I promise.

# The Honey Cake Mix-Up

As soon as Pooh and Roo got home, Pooh mixed the Tigger-lilies with the other ingredients.

Pooh let Roo stir for a while. Then he poured the mixture into a pan.

Before Pooh put the pan in the oven, Roo said, "It looks kind of funny."

Pooh stared at the lumpy orange mixture. "That's because it's not cooked," he said. "It will look different once we bake it."

**P**ooh has promised to help his good friend Roo with something very special — baking a cake for Roo's mom, Kanga — and what could be tastier than a honey cake? The two friends diligently bake their cake, but it proves to be a soggy disappointment. What went wrong? Helpful Rabbit enlightens the pair of eager bakers by telling them they forgot the *flour* — but Pooh and Roo hear *flower* instead. And so they begin their fruitless but hilarious search for just the right flower to make their cake perfect.

As the well-meaning Pooh and Roo are helped by their friends, they learn that words that sound the same don't always have the same meaning. All's well that ends well as Kanga receives a lovely, fragrant honey cake and sweet-scented roses from Christopher Robin's garden. The misadventures of Pooh and Roo will teach children that:

🐝 different words can sound alike.

🐝 doing nice things for others makes you feel good, too.

🐝 tenacity makes things possible.

🐝 baking together can be fun.

## What's It All About?

Small children's vocabularies will quickly increase if they chat with adults. Start a conversation by asking questions about the story they've read. Help your child with the answers so he won't feel pressure to perform. Ask the following questions matter-of-factly and let your child take his time answering:

- Why did Roo want to bake a cake?
- What kind of cake did Pooh and Roo want to bake?
- Why wouldn't thistles be good in a cake?
- What kind of flowers grew in Christopher Robin's garden?

## Thinking Time

Developing a child's thinking skills before he begins school will give him a head start. And when children learn to imagine "What if?" "Why?" and other questions that build analytical and reasoning strengths, creativity blossoms. Try these:

- What do you think your mother or father would like for a birthday surprise?
- What would you like for a birthday surprise?
- Why do you think Pooh wanted to help Roo make the honey cake?

## Kanga's Honey Cake

Here is a recipe for a honey cake that parents and children can make together. As you measure each ingredient, discuss with your child its purpose, for example, honey makes the cake sweet, eggs hold the batter together and make it fluffy, butter helps bind the batter and gives the cake flavor, baking soda and baking powder make the cake rise. Mix together: 3 eggs, 1 cup sugar, 1 cup honey, 1 teaspoon baking powder, 1 lemon (grated rind and juice), 1/2 cup oil or softened butter, 3/4 cup water or milk. Add 1 teaspoon baking soda and 2 cups flour. Mix all well with a wooden spoon and pour into a greased and floured loaf pan. Bake at 375°F for 45 minutes or until cake springs back to the touch. Cool and slice.

## Bubble, Bubble, No Toil, No Trouble

Showing your child how baking soda makes cakes rise is a first lesson in chemistry. Pour about a teaspoon of baking soda into a small dish of water. Ask your child to describe the reaction. Don't worry about delving into the intricacies of chemistry and chemical reactions; just say that something called a chemical makes it bubble. Explain that the bubbles make air in the cake and force it to rise. Discuss what a cake would be like without the baking soda.

# Eeyore's Happy Tail

Tigger went around to the other end of Eeyore and looked at his tail. "I think I see the problem," he reported back. "We'll have you fixed up in no time."

He gave Eeyore's tail a good crinkling. Then he folded it up and called out to Eeyore, "Okay, you're all set. Now lean back, and before you know it, you'll be bouncin', just like me!"

**E**eyore dreams of being the complete opposite of the sad, glum donkey he really is: happy, outgoing, funny, entertaining, and someone with whom others want to be. But when his dream ends, Eeyore is sadder than ever, wishing he were really the other Eeyore. When happy Tigger bounces by, Eeyore notices his tail is crinkly and cheerful. Searching for the perfect tail to change his personality, Eeyore learns about the tails of other animals. And when he finally finds the perfect one, he discovers that he was just right the way he was. Eeyore's story will teach children that:

🐝 you should be happy with the person you are.
🐝 animals have different uses for their tails.
🐝 true friends like you the way you are.
🐝 you don't have to be the life of the party to be loved.
🐝 good friends will tell you the truth.

## What's It All About?

As children are exposed to more and more books, they will be able not only to relate what happens in sequence, but to begin detecting changes in plot development and outcomes. This growing sophistication can be developed by asking questions that relate to these important elements of any story. The following questions will help:

• How did Eeyore feel about his dream?
• Whose tail did Eeyore admire?
• What animals' tails did Eeyore learn about?

- What kind of tail did Owl pin to Eeyore?
- What did Christopher Robin say about Eeyore's old tail?

## Thinking Time

Introduce your child to the idea of opinions. Practice with opinion questions such as "What's the best ice cream in the world?" and when she answers, tell her your favorite. Which one is right? Both, of course. This helps your child understand that her opinions are valued and that people see things differently and have different perspectives. Try these thinking questions to get started:

- Why do you think Eeyore wanted to be different from the way he really was?
- Why do you think Owl is so smart?
- Why did Christopher Robin like Eeyore's tail just the way it was?

## Tell a Joke, Sing a Song

Eeyore wanted to be entertaining for his friends. Teach your child some simple jokes and have her repeat them for you and the family in the evening. If you've forgotten them, there are lots of joke books available in the children's section of the local library. Teach your child familiar songs such as "Row, Row, Row Your Boat," "The Farmer in the Dell," and "This Old Man." Telling jokes and singing songs makes children more poised and self-assured, and increases memory and listening skills.

## Make Some Tails

Make a monkey's tail, a beaver's tail, and a peacock's tail. Color them appropriately, and review why each animal has the type of tail that it does. Help your child affix each tail to her clothing and pretend to be that animal. Make Tigger's crinkly tail and encourage your child to bounce!

## I Can Be Christopher Robin

Have your child pretend to be Christopher Robin with all her animal friends. (This will give new life to your child's neglected stuffed animals as well!) Gather the animals together and help your child make up a story about herself and her toys as they come to life in her imagination. Illustrate the story. She'll want to make up more!

# There's No Place Like Home

Roo hopped back to Kanga as fast as he could. She kissed him and helped him into her pouch. Then she gave him a pat and bounded off.

Inside, Roo smiled sleepily. He wasn't a dandelion, or a coconut, or a cocklebur. His friends had helped him to find that out. But he was Roo, with lots to see from his mama's pouch, and lots of room to grow.

**R**OO has been given a free ride in his mother Kanga's pouch since the day he was born. Now he thinks it's time to strike out on his own, leave the pouch, and become independent. He discovers by observing different kinds of seeds that there are many ways to travel, and with the help of his friends, he tries them all. But in the end, Roo discovers that there's only one perfect way to see the world for a little kangaroo like him, and that's from his mama's warm, safe pouch. Roo's story will teach children that:

🐝 the world is different outside their home.

🐝 friends can help you satisfy your curiosity about the world.

🐝 seeds are interesting to observe and you can learn from them.

🐝 hobbies, such as collecting things, can be shared with others.

🐝 friends can help you learn about yourself.

🐝 it's important to appreciate your home.

## What's It All About?

Comprehension is an important component in learning to read. Words read well and ideas understood make for a competent reader now and throughout your child's life. Ask questions gently. You might begin with

"First, Roo was in Kanga's pouch. Hmmm. Who is Kanga?" There's a good chance your child will shout or giggle, "She's his mother, silly!" Note the use of the word "first." This leads to sequencing of events, which helps children become organized and understand chronological order. Early understanding of this will not only help them retell a story correctly, but will enable children to later write their own stories in sequential order. Try these questions:

- After Roo left Kanga's pouch, who did he meet first?
- What was Rabbit doing when Roo met him?
- What kind of collection did Rabbit have?
- What happened to the balloon?
- What did Kanga do when Roo returned?

## Thinking Time

More and more educators are emphasizing that children need to be able to think and to solve problems in order to function in the world of the future. Ask your child questions that prompt him to consider everything he knows about a subject, then encourage him to reach a logical conclusion. Try these questions to get started:

- Why do you think Roo wanted to leave Kanga's nice, warm pouch?
- If you could go out on your own, where would you like to go? Why?
- What did Roo find out from the seeds?

## What Belongs Together?

Classification is an excellent skill that can be expanded and extended into many areas. And it's easy! Go through your child's toy box, or even your kitchen's small-utensils drawer. Choose some objects randomly and spread them out on the floor or on a table. Ask your child, "What's the same

about these?" and provide enough time for him to separate them according to what strikes him. The child might choose to place all the small items, or blue items, or things that have the same shape or are made of the same material together. It's also a great game for a children's party!

## Things That Float, Things That Sink

Remind your child that Rabbit showed Roo that coconuts float. Collect items such as a rock, a piece of paper, a small rubber ball, a feather, a rubber duckie, and, yes, a coconut. Place them one at a time in a bucket or tub or bowl. Name which ones float and which ones sink. Help your child try to figure out why this is so. Your child's guesses don't have to be correct — the key is to encourage thinking.

# Fun Is Where You Find It

After Pooh had left, Rabbit picked up his rake and headed for the maple tree to do more work. On the way, he saw a leaf floating in the breeze. Rabbit wondered what it was like to be a leaf. He knew what his friend Pooh would do if he were here.

Rabbit dropped his rake, and began chasing the leaf through the forest. "My goodness," thought Rabbit, "fall is fun!"

It's fall, and Rabbit is not at all happy about raking the leaves that have covered his yard. To him, fall means hard work. When Pooh happens by, Rabbit patiently explains why the trees drop their leaves, and soon the two friends find themselves on a fall adventure. Pooh delights in each discovery, especially a fat, round pumpkin that resembles his chubby tummy. The two chance upon a squirrel and some lovely, shiny red apples. By journey's end, Pooh has shown Rabbit that fall can be fun! This upbeat story shows children that:

🦋 imagination can make almost any experience fun.

🦋 friends can teach each other wonderful things.

🦋 many exciting changes happen in the fall.

🦋 exploring your environment can bring delightful surprises.

## What's It All About?

This story explores work and fun. Ask your child to give examples of what she considers hard work, then give your own. Discuss how something she might consider hard work, you might consider fun, and vice versa. Now ask her questions that help her recall Pooh's and Rabbit's fall adventure:

• What job made Rabbit feel sad?
• The pumpkin reminded Pooh of something. What?
• What did Pooh do with the apples he found?
• What kind of scarf did Pooh want to wear?

## Thinking Time

To get your child in a thinking mood, talk about fall in your area. Is it similar to fall in the Hundred-Acre Wood, or different? Then try these questions:

- Why didn't Rabbit like fall?
- Why couldn't Pooh talk with the apples in his mouth?
- Why did Rabbit decide that fall wasn't so bad after all?
- Why do you think Pooh liked fall so much?

## Leaf Prints and Stained-Glass Leaves

This easy art activity will delight children. Collect leaves in any season. Arrange the leaves in a pleasing pattern, veins up, then place tissue or newsprint paper over the leaves. Help children rub the paper with leaf-colored crayons. Or place leaves between two sheets of waxed paper (wax side facing the leaves), and iron them together with a warm iron. Tape the picture in a sunny window for maximum effect.

## Animals in the Fall

Get some books from the library or a bookstore about various animals and discuss with your child which animals get ready for the winter. Read *The Grasshopper and the Ants* and other fables that tell about animal behavior. Talk about why bears might hibernate and why they don't have to eat for most of the winter. Do some thinking exercises, discussing what it would be like if people stored food for the winter or hibernated.

## Pumpkin Poems

You and your child can have fun making up a pumpkin poem. Cut out pumpkins from orange construction paper. With marker or crayon, make faces on them according to the rhyme below. Help your child learn the rhyme and perhaps make up additional verses.

This is a pumpkin that's happy,
This is a pumpkin that's sad,
This is a pumpkin that's silly,
This is a pumpkin that's mad.

## Short Stories

Help your child create a simple fall story using the following vocabulary words: harvest, blustery, gaze, scarf, pile, frown, tummy, maple, and tree. Write the sentences your child dictates to you on lined paper and then have your child illustrate them. Gather everyone around after dinner for "story time," during which you and your child can read her latest work!

# Sweet Dreams

Pooh looked at the snapdragon again. Suddenly he knew just what to do.
Spreading his wings, he flew into the air and buzzed around the flower. Why hadn't he noticed how sweet snapdragons smelled before? He took a deep breath, then landed on a petal.

**P**ooh has exhausted his supply of honey. He pursues some bees in search of more and, accompanied by Piglet, finds himself in Rabbit's garden. Rabbit soon explains to them how bees make the sticky stuff. It's an interesting story, but Pooh still wants honey, and thinking about how to get some is tiring for a bear of little brain. Soon Pooh is fast asleep, dreaming that he is a bee, flying from flower to flower, lapping up sweet nectar. Upon awakening, Pooh is refreshed and ready to think of new ways to get that honey — and looking forward to the next sweet dream. Pooh's story will teach children that:

- honey comes from bees, and bees make it from nectar.
- dreams can be fun to remember and to talk about.
- friends can help you pursue your goals.
- determination and tenacity can be rewarding.

## What's It All About?

Turn the tables and encourage your child to ask *you* questions about the story. Deliberately answer some incorrectly so he can correct you. This will build self-esteem while giving your child the feeling that he's participating. Not only that, but he'll have fun quizzing mom or dad. Start with these questions:

- What happened to Pooh's honey?
- Who helped Pooh look for honey?
- In whose garden did Pooh and Piglet find themselves?
- What did Pooh turn into in his dream?

## Thinking Time

Now expand on thinking skills by asking questions with answers that are open-ended. For example, "Why do you think Mommy or Daddy goes to work each day? Why is it fun to read?" Use the following book-related questions to further improve creative brainwork:

- Why do you think Pooh dreamed about bees and honey?
- Why do you think bees build their hives in high trees?
- Why do you think Pooh liked his dream?

## Buzzy Bees

What noise do bees make? Encourage your child to make buzzy bee sounds, then continue with sounds that other animals make. Your child will enjoy wearing a makeshift bee suit. Make a yellow and black paper or fabric bee suit and a paper or felt stinger. Gather some flowers and show your child where the nectar is stored.

## Honey Pot Game

Use a big pot or kettle from the kitchen for this game. Help your child draw, color, and cut ten little honeybees out of paper. Put numbers from one to ten on the bees and put them in the pot. Take turns choosing a bee. Whenever your child identifies the number correctly, he gets to keep the bee. At the end of the game, whoever has the most bees wins a small reward. For variety, write letters or simple words on the bees.

## Buttercups and Other Strange Things

Ask your child to draw what he thinks a buttercup might look like. He might picture a cup full of butter or a cup made of butter. Show your child an illustration of a buttercup. Tell him there are also flowers called snapdragons and Johnny-jump-ups. Discuss what they might look like.

## Vocabulary Ladder

On a large piece of paper, draw a tall tree, with a hive at the top and a ladder against it. On each rung of the ladder write a vocabulary word. Read each word with your child, then see if he can read them back to you, climbing the ladder rung by rung. When he reaches the top, provide a small reward. Vocabulary ideas: honey, bee, tree, lunch, pot, tummy.

# Weather or Not

Finally they were able to open their eyes. Pooh looked at the grass swaying gently in the breeze and said, "It's more breezy than windy now. Why don't we fly kites?"

"What kites?" Piglet asked.

"The ones we can make with our napkins," Pooh said. "I got the idea when I saw your napkin blow away."

**P**ooh feels like going on a picnic, and checks out the weather report with Owl first. Owl tells him that no precipitation or wind is expected, so Pooh rounds up some friends to share a picnic. But "presipping" and wind are definitely on the menu. Undaunted, the clever friends make kites to fly in the wind, and batten down the blanket with honey pots. A good time is had by all because any day is a fun one as long as you spend it with friends. This story will teach children that:

- being flexible leads to fun times.
- it's fun to learn new words such as "precipitation."
- you can use things on hand to be creative (such as napkins and sticks to make kites).
- weather forecasts aren't always accurate!
- even bad weather is fun to share with friends.

## What's It All About?

One method of getting a child excited about a new book is to read it first, then tell the child, "I just read a nice book and I want to share it with you." Your child will be pleased that you're spending time with her and look forward to the reading. You might give her a synopsis of part of the book, then stop and say, "But I don't want to spoil it for you. Let's read it together and find out what happens." This works with any child, but is particularly effective with children who are reluctant readers.

Here are some comprehension questions to ask when the book is finished:

- Whom did Pooh invite on the picnic?
- What did Pooh and his friends bring to eat?
- How did Pooh make a kite?
- Who felt the rain first?
- What did Pooh use to hold down the blanket?

## Thinking Time

Answering thinking questions will make your child as creative as Pooh and his friends were. Use the questions below as a beginning point. As your child's skill increases in answering thinking questions, make up some of your own, raising the level of difficulty a bit.

- Why do you think the weather report is sometimes wrong?
- Why is it fun to have a picnic?
- Why did the friends have fun even though it rained?

## Spring Cleaning

Discuss with your child what spring cleaning is. Tell her it can be accomplished in any season. Ask her to choose a closet, drawer, or small area to help you clean. This is an excellent opportunity to teach your child how to dust, polish, and tuck away things in their proper places, helping her form lifelong habits of responsibility, cleanliness, and neatness. Play the Spring Cleaning Game, too. From magazines or other sources, cut out items that would be found in each room of a house. Mix them up, then have your child sort them out in boxes you provide labeled kitchen, bathroom,

bedroom, dining room, or whichever rooms are appropriate for your home. Label the items if you wish to increase your child's reading vocabulary.

## I Went on a Picnic . . .

This is a great game to increase auditory memory: Say "I went on a picnic and I brought chocolate cake." Your child must repeat what you said and add a selection of her own: "I went on a picnic and I brought chocolate cake and tuna sandwiches." Limit the list to five items, and only increase the number if your child is having fun with the game.

## Picnic Memories

This promotes visual discrimination. Draw or cut out pictures of picnic items and glue them to a piece of paper. Tell your child she can look at them until you count to ten. After you've counted, turn the paper upside down and ask her to recall what she saw.

# The Perfect Pet

of the Hundred-Acre Wood. Soon it was joined by other butterflies, brightening the sky.

From then on, whenever Eeyore was lonely, he would think of all those beautiful butterflies, flying out there somewhere, and he wouldn't feel alone anymore.

Eeyore shook his head sadly and said, "I've lost my perfect pet, haven't I?"

"Yes," said Christopher Robin, "but look at how beautiful it is now."

The butterfly spread its wings and rose into the air. As Eeyore watched, it floated over the flowers and meadows

**E**eyore is lonely and dreams about having a pet. He considers several but decides they're too much work. He finds the perfect pet — a caterpillar. But Eeyore is dismayed when his little friend becomes a brown lump. Christopher Robin gently explains to the little donkey how caterpillars make cocoons before they change into something wonderful. Eeyore is thrilled when he sees his friend become a beautiful butterfly and join other butterflies happily flitting about in the sky. This story will teach children that:

🦋 pets are fun but also mean work and responsibility.

🦋 it takes some research to find the perfect pet.

🦋 caterpillars change into butterflies.

## What's It All About?

Sooner or later your child will want a pet. Talk about pets he knows, and what he thinks would be fun or not so fun about having them. If your child already has a pet, ask him what he likes best and least about having it. This will help him sympathize with Eeyore's feelings.

Then try these questions for enrichment of the story:

- Who is the gray boat with floppy ears?
- Why didn't Eeyore want a dog?
- What did Eeyore like about his caterpillar?
- What happened to Eeyore's pet caterpillar?

## Thinking Time

Sometimes children experience loneliness. Encourage your child to talk about these feelings, and how there are sometimes things you can do to make them go away. (For example, at night, take a stuffed animal to bed; during the day, find activities to enjoy alone.) Then discuss the questions below:

- Why do you think Eeyore was lonely?
- Why would a pet make Eeyore feel happy?
- Why do you think the butterfly flew away when Eeyore tried to catch it?

## Play Poohsticks

After you've read the book, come up with your own version of Poohsticks. Collect some sticks, then put them on the ground about one foot apart. Direct your child to jump between the sticks without stepping on them to win a reward. Or gather some fat sticks and write numbers on them from one to ten. Scatter them about and ask your child to arrange them on the ground in order. Or how about a game of "Pick Up Poohsticks"? Provide six sticks, then ask your child to bounce a ball and, while doing so, to pick up a stick. Put the stick in a box and have your child repeat until all the sticks have been picked up.

## Pets of Many Faces

Help your child create simple masks of animals that could be pets. Make the masks out of construction paper and tie them on with string. Or make paper bag puppets instead. Draw and cut out various animal or bird heads, then glue each to the bottom of a paper sandwich bag. Encourage your child to put on a funny play, making up dialogue for his creations.

## Butterflies Flutter By

Children will love making these colorful butterflies and pretending to be one of them. Look for pictures of butterflies in magazines, books, or other sources. Help your child draw free-form butterflies on large pieces of construction paper, butcher paper, or other sturdy paper. Show him how to draw markings and colorful wings with bright crayons.

Butterflies can be made in several layers and glued together if you and your child wish to have more elaborate "pets." Cut them out. Staple rubber bands to the undersides of the butterflies and put the rubber bands around your child's wrists. Have him run about, flapping his arms and pretending to fly.

# Cozy Beds

When he went to bed each night, Eeyore would think about the animals Kanga had told them about. Wherever they were, Eeyore knew that just like them, he had a cozy bed all his own.

Which is how Eeyore came to spend the long winter nights at Pooh's house — with Roo staying for a sleep-over every now and then.

Pooh and Roo go to the pond to play, but winter has begun, and the water has turned to ice. They enjoy sliding on the ice but end up smacking into a snowbank. Surprise! The snowbank turns out to be Eeyore covered with snow. His twig house has blown away in the wind, and he needs a cozy place to rest. The friends are concerned about where their gloomy friend will go, and with the help of Kanga they explore the places and ways in which animals sleep during the winter. Finally, Pooh invites Eeyore to spend the long winter at his house. This story teaches children that:

🐾 animals have many different ways of spending the winter.

🐾 everyone needs a cozy bed in which to sleep.

🐾 friends help each other.

🐾 water turns to ice in cold weather.

### What's It All About?

To reinforce reading comprehension, ask your child how each animal mentioned in the story behaves in winter. Then hone in on what Pooh and his friends do with the following questions:

• Why did Pooh decide it was time to get up?

• What did Pooh and Roo pretend to be?

• Why couldn't Eeyore sleep in his house?

• What are two animals that don't sleep all winter?

## Thinking Time

Get your child thinking about how people and animals adapt to the weather. For example, ask her what people can do to stay warm in the winter. Then follow up with these related questions:

- Why did Pooh wrap a scarf around his neck?
- What do you think *peaceful* means?
- Why did Pooh think everything was so peaceful after it snowed?
- Why did Pooh want Eeyore to stay at his house?

## It's Freezing!

This is a great experiment to introduce your child to the wonders and practicality of science. Place warm water in a shallow dish. Have your child put her hand in the water. Talk about how it feels. Repeat this with cooler water. Take the dish and put it in the freezer. Remove it several times: when it gets cold, when ice begins to form, and when ice becomes solid. See if your child can make the connection that the colder the water, the closer it gets to turning into ice.

Reverse the experiment by allowing the ice to defrost, and help your child deduce what is happening. Talk about the uses of ice.

## A House for Eeyore

Eeyore can't stay at Pooh's house forever, so help your child design a new one that won't blow away. On a big piece of paper, draw a house, decide the materials needed for it, and determine how to design it so it won't blow down. Label each part of the house, then draw Eeyore, who will live in it. Discuss each phase of this activity: What can we do so the house won't blow down? What makes a house blow down? What makes a house strong? What makes a house cozy? To extend this activity, draw the inside of the house and all its furniture, custom-made for a small donkey. Better still, actually build the house you've designed using wood, cardboard, or other household materials.

## Meet-a-Squirrel Game

Invite your child to "meet a squirrel" by helping her get to the top of a vocabulary tree. Take a long piece of paper and draw a tree with a squirrel sitting in the top. Write the following words going up the tree: nest, cozy, squirrel, raccoon, scarf, ice, snow, mouse, moth, donkey. Toss one die to determine how many words your child can "climb." She must say each word when she comes to it in order to keep going. Help her when necessary so she can successfully reach the squirrel.

# A Wonderful Wind

The friends hopped aboard. Christopher Robin steered the boat so the wind could fill the sails. In no time, the sailboat was gliding across the water.
Pooh turned to Piglet and asked, "Is it too breezy for you?"

"I'm fine," said Piglet. "As long as I hold on tight, I probably won't fly away."
Pooh moved closer and put his arm around his friend.
"I won't let you go," he said reassuringly.

It's a wonderfully blustery day, but Piglet is much too afraid of the wind to appreciate it. With the help of his friends, Piglet discovers that wind flies kites, helps spiders travel, and turns pinwheels. The friends use the wind to go sailing, then join Kanga and Owl for a tea party. By that time, Piglet is so excited about his windy discoveries that he even suggests that they open a window and enjoy the breeze. This story teaches children that:

- investigating fears can make fears disappear.
- playing with pinwheels and flying kites is fun.
- things that are light are whisked into the air by the wind.
- wind pushes the sails on boats and helps birds fly.
- wind circulates smells, good and bad.

## What's It All About?

Tell the story out of sequence to see if your child is able to correct you. Make your errors big ones, so they can be easily spotted, enabling your child to feel successful.

Then try these questions:
- What was Piglet's dream?
- Who did the wind take into the air first?
- What was Christopher Robin's idea?
- Why did the friends get stuck in the boat?

## Thinking Time

To make thinking fun, draw a light bulb on a piece of cardboard and give it to your child. The moment he has an answer to one of these thinking questions, tell him to hold up the card!

- Why can the wind be scary?
- Why was it too windy to garden, according to Rabbit?
- Why was Owl worried about Eeyore?
- Why do you think we need the wind?

## Make a Pinwheel!

Take a colorful piece of not-too-heavy paper, such as a piece of colored photocopying paper. Cut it into a six-inch square. (The pinwheel must be square, all sides equal in length, or it won't work properly.) Cut four diagonal slits — one from each corner — stopping about one inch short of the center. Fold over, rolling each corner a bit (see illustration). Stick a brass paper fastener in the center and fasten it to a dowel or through a plastic straw. Cover rough edges of fastener with tape. Ask your child how to get the pinwheel to move. Blow the pinwheel together, then take it outside to see if the wind will spin it. For further experimentation, hold it in front of a fan.

## Fly Away

Use the wind or a fan for this fun experiment. Make a collection of items to see if they are light enough for the wind to lift. Explain to your child that wind is *moving air*. Use things such as feathers, small pieces of paper, ribbon, and some heavier things such as pencils and even rocks.

## What's That Smell?

Place some smelly things such as cheese, onions, garlic, and perfume in front of an electric fan. Place a blindfold over your child's eyes and turn on the fan. Ask him to identify the smells.

## Can You See the Wind?

Ask your child if he can see the wind. He may say that he can see the leaves blow. Explain that he is seeing what the wind *does*, not the wind itself. Talk about other things that you know are there but you can't see: air, sounds, temperature.

Now play an imagination game. Ask your child, "If you could see the wind, what color would it be?" Encourage him to draw a picture of what the wind would look like if it were a person, and ask him what it would say.

Also suggest that your child pretend to be different objects being blown by the wind. Ask him to show you how a feather caught in the wind would act differently than a piece of paper would.

# Rain, Rain, Come Again

"We'll keep looking, then," said Pooh, who wasn't looking, and fell into a great big puddle.
"Here, let me help," offered Piglet, who instantly fell in.

Soon Eeyore and Piglet both slipped in, too. Since they were already wet, the friends decided to enjoy a game of puddle-jumping.
"Whee!" cried Roo, who was having so much fun he didn't seem to notice the water splashing on his head.

**P**ooh and his friends decide to discover a new land, which they will name after themselves. But when rain threatens, Eeyore and Roo are not so sure they should go. The group sets out anyway and gets caught in the rain, meets earthworms, and sees a bee in the clouds. They do find a place they haven't seen before, but decide it's not grand enough to bear their names. They've had so much fun, though, that they look forward to going exploring another day — preferably a rainy one! This story will teach young children that:

🐝 it's fun to explore new places.

🐝 although your plans may not work out exactly the way you'd hoped, you can still have fun.

🐝 a compass helps you know where you are.

🐝 even a rainy day can be fun.

## What's It All About?

After your child has answered the comprehension questions below, suggest to her that she retell the story to a friend or relative. This will raise self-esteem and enable your child to realize that others consider her reading important too.

- Where did the friends want to go on their Explore at first?
- After they met Eeyore, what did they decide to name their land?
- What happened to their map?
- Why did the worms come out?

- What did Roo want before he went to bed?

## Thinking Time

"Put on your thinking cap" is an old-fashioned way to tell children to start thinking. You might even provide a special hat or cap that your child will keep for this purpose. Then try these questions:

- Why would it be fun to find a new land?
- Why did the friends decide to name their new land after all of them?
- Why do you think the map didn't work as protection from the rain?
- Why did Kanga think tea and cookies would make the friends feel better?

## Rain, Rain, Stay Off Me!

Have a "brainstorming" session with your child on the best ways to keep dry if she were caught in a downpour. Her first answer will probably be "an umbrella." Accept that answer, then tell her there are no umbrellas to be found. Discuss what characteristics something to shelter her from the rain would need. Help her draw pictures of how she would stay dry.

## Let's Explore!

After reading this book, your child will be eager to go on an Explore to find uncharted places. Suggest that you explore the house first, then the yard, then take her on a walk in an unfamiliar park, or neighborhood, or even a neighbor's yard. Have her name the place for herself and other members of the family. When you return home, have her record the Explore, with drawings of where you went and words that tell about what she saw and did.

## Heffalumps and Woozles Were Here!

Talk about what heffalumps and woozles might look like. Draw their footprints with colored chalk on the sidewalk. Have the footprints lead somewhere (such as to your house, with milk and cookies waiting), and have your child invite a friend or two to follow the footprints and claim the reward.

## Word Walk

Write vocabulary words and numbers from one to ten on heavy paper or cardboard and cut them out to resemble rocks or earthworms. Scatter them about in your house, on a porch, or in the yard. Ask your child to gather the "rocks" or "worms." Provide a small reward for the discovery. Suggested words: bucket, map, ink, rain, mud, tummy, worm, puddle.

# Eeyore's Lucky Day

Eeyore looked at Christopher Robin, then Pooh, then Rabbit and Piglet and Tigger. He was not used to so many good things happening to him at once.

Finally he said, "I don't know if four-leaf clovers really work, but I know that I'm lucky to have you as friends." "We're lucky to have each other," said Pooh. "Yes, Pooh," said Christopher Robin as he patted Eeyore on the head. "We are."

**G**lum Eeyore is convinced that his usual bad luck has struck once again when his house blows down and he gets stuck in the mud. However, being the greatest of friends, Pooh and company band together to change the donkey's luck by finding him a four-leaf clover. When one is finally found, Eeyore's luck does change. As he thinks about it, though, Eeyore realizes that his true luck is having such loyal, caring friends. Eeyore's story will teach children about:

- helping friends.
- how working together and not giving up bring results.
- how good it feels to help others and see their joy.
- the power of positive thinking.

## What's It All About?

Your child will probably wonder what four-leaf clovers are, as they are uncommon indeed! Before you begin to read the book, draw a clover and ask your child to color it green, then cut it out. He can hang onto it while you're reading the book, and use it as a bookmark later. Adding this visual touch will help with reading comprehension. Having some paper ready to draw simple illustrations will again help your child to visualize and remember the story. Try these questions:

- Why did Eeyore's house blow down?
- What is Eeyore's favorite food?
- What did Tigger do to the four-leaf clover?
- Name all of Eeyore's friends.
- How did Eeyore get a new house?

## Thinking Time

Even young children can formulate ideas, draw conclusions, and predict outcomes if they are guided to do so. Start simply. Perhaps you're walking in the park and see a squirrel collecting and running away with nuts or seeds. You might pose the question: "Why doesn't the squirrel sit and eat all the nuts now?" Also try these questions about the story:

- Why do you think Eeyore is sad all the time?
- If you could make a wish on a four-leaf clover, what would you wish?
- What could Eeyore do so his house doesn't blow over in the wind again?
- Why is Eeyore lucky to have friends?

## You Can Count on It!

The world is full of things to count! Eeyore and his friends count clover leaves. Remind your child about the clover leaves, then suggest you count some things together. Start with items that go to five, then ten, and go on as far as your child can without becoming frustrated or bored. Children learn to count at different ages and stages, so keep it fun for both of you. A few things your child might have fun counting: balloons, crayons, fingers and toes, cousins, types of toys, keys on your keychain.

## Treasure Hunt!

Have a treasure hunt starting with the four-leaf clover you made before you read this book. Make a list of five things to find together that will take you throughout the house. Read the list to your child. (This is a great way to emphasize classification skills, sequence, and organization.) For example: something for cooking, something soft to sit upon, something to read, something that makes noise, something that smells good. Give a small prize when everything is collected.

## Help Eeyore Build His House

Eeyore's house was made of sticks. Your child will have fun making a new house for him using (Popsicle-type) craft sticks and glue. This is excellent for "building" hand-eye coordination. Try to resist the temptation to take over and become the chief architect. Instead, encourage your child to discover what shapes and styles of buildings would make a good house for a donkey.

# Rabbit's Ears

Alone at last, Rabbit began picking corn. Suddenly, the sweet silence was interrupted by a loud TAP TAP TAP! Rabbit whirled around, wondering who would dare ignore his sign.

Again he heard TAP TAP TAP!
   Finally Rabbit looked up in a tree. "Oh, no!" he said. "It's a woodpecker!"
   As the woodpecker continued tapping, Rabbit covered his ears. To his dismay, he could still hear TAP TAP TAP!

Rabbit relishes the peace and quiet that surround him as he pulls weeds one summer day. But it doesn't last long as, one by one, his friends disrupt his thinking time with chatter, noise, and lots of what Rabbit considers bothersome interruptions. Very much annoyed, Rabbit seeks ways to shut out the noise of his friends, and although he succeeds, he discovers that he's also missing out on lots of things that are important to hear. He wisely decides that quiet time is nice, but being with friends is even nicer. Rabbit's story will teach children that:

- quiet time is important, but not all time should be quiet time.
- being sociable can lead to fun.
- the world is full of noises — and many are important to hear.
- be careful what you wish for — you might get it!

## What's It All About?

As you read the story, encourage your child to act out what is happening. For example, ask her to "pull" weeds, pretend to take a nap, or make a sign. Then see how much she remembered by asking these questions:

- What was Rabbit doing on a summer day?
- What was the racket that Tigger and Roo were making?
- What did Rabbit's sign say?
- What two ways did Rabbit use to shut out the noise?
- What did Rabbit's friends almost do without him?

## Thinking Time

Ask your child to describe what thinking is. Discuss whether it is possible to *not* think. This activity will naturally lead to these thought-provoking questions:

- Why do people like to think?
- Why is it often helpful to be in a quiet place instead of a noisy one when you're thinking?
- When do you like to have quiet time?
- Why did Rabbit decide that it was okay for his friends to make noise, after all?

## Problems and Solutions

Rabbit solved his noise problem by trial and error. First he used earmuffs, and when they didn't work, he put cotton in his ears. Discuss the following problems with your child and how they could be solved. Help her point out why each solution might or might not work. The problems and solutions below are examples, but make up your own to fit your environment.

*Problem:* Friends mess up her room when they come to play.

*Possible solutions:* Take out only one or two toys at a time, then put them away; show the friends where the toys go.

## It Makes Sense

Discuss the five senses (sight, hearing, touch, smell, taste) with your child and, over several days, play games to reinforce each one. Games might include having your child close her eyes and then remember what she saw in the room, making different noises with articles found around the house and having your child identify them without looking, having your child touch and taste different foods with her eyes closed and then asking her to describe them.

## All Kinds of Noise

Help your child make a list of things that make noise, and things that don't. Ask her to make as many of the noises as she can. Challenge her by suggesting some sounds that require imagination. Can she make the sound of a growing flower? Of falling snow? Of a floating feather?

## Name That Sound

Tape-record a variety of everyday sounds, such as birds singing, a car starting, a faucet dripping, or a ball bouncing. Choose some sounds that are easy to identify, and others that are more difficult. Then make a game of playing the tape and asking your child to identify each sound. Make the activity more challenging by asking "What kind of bird is singing?" or "Is the ball that's bouncing big or small?" Add more players for even more fun.

# The Bug Hunt

A while later Christopher Robin returned, and the friends divided up the jars and butterfly nets. As Tiger slung his net over his shoulder, he proclaimed, "Bug hunting is what Tiggers do best!"

So Roo begged to go bug-hunting with Tigger, and Piglet quickly chose Pooh for a partner. Christopher Robin and Kanga paired off, which left Rabbit to team up with Owl. Eeyore remained under the tree.

Owl inspires his friends to collect insects, and they all decide to go on a bug hunt. Everyone chooses a partner and sets off with nets and jars. As the excitement grows over the variety of bugs they find, Rabbit and Owl begin to argue. They disagree about how to catch them, where to find them, and who should keep the bugs. They finish by catching nothing, while their friends catch ladybugs, a dragonfly, and a grasshopper. As they set the bugs free, the friends are treated to a nighttime show of sparkling firefly lights, and the bickering is forgotten. This story teaches children that:

- insects are interesting.
- it's fun to go on a bug hunt with friends.
- you shouldn't hurt bugs, but release them after you enjoy them for a little while.
- friends can waste a lot of time arguing over silly things.
- a butterfly collector is called a lepidopterist.

## What's It All About?

Young children love to learn "grown-up" words such as "lepidopterist." Introduce them to others, such as "philatelist" (someone who collects stamps) and "numismatist" (someone who collects coins). They'll love showing off by pronouncing these words for family and friends! Then continue to challenge them with these comprehension questions:

- What does a lepidopterist do?

- How did the friends pair up?
- What do ladybugs eat?
- What is special about fireflies?

## Thinking Time

Reading between the lines and understanding feelings and motives of characters will enrich your child's enjoyment of literature. Try these questions to kick off discussion:
- Why did Rabbit and Owl argue?
- Why might it be fun to collect bugs?
- Why should you be careful when collecting bugs?
- Why did Roo want to bug-hunt with Tigger?

## Let's Go Bug-Hunting!

After reading this story, your child will be raring to go on a real bug hunt. Fortunately, bugs are all around us. The only equipment needed is a container in which to keep the bugs. Make sure it's not glass and that it has many holes in it so the insects can breathe. A good container is a carton from take-out Chinese food. Cut out a "window" in the front of the container and tape a piece of clear plastic or plastic wrap over the square so that the bugs can be observed.

Explain to your child that bugs can't live without food and need to be free, so keep the collection for a short time, then release the bugs where they were found. Emphasize respect for all living creatures.

## Invent-a-Bug

Give your child a big piece of paper and suggest that he create a new type of bug. What is different about this bug? Does it talk? Does it clean rooms? Does it mow the lawn? Provide some ideas and help your child design his fantasy bug. Create one out of a household sponge, using pipe cleaners for legs and antennae. Make sure the bug has six legs, though—basic for bugs.

## Arguing for Fun

Your child will be involved in arguments at an early age, having conflicts with friends about toys, games, and a variety of other issues. Discuss the disagreement between Rabbit and Owl and how it was resolved. Do some role-playing with your child. Have him play one role while you play the other, then switch.

Set up these imaginary situations: Your friend breaks your favorite toy, and that makes you angry; you don't want to finish your dinner, but your mom or dad wants you to; your friend wants to change the rules of a game, but you like them the way they are. Make up situations that are pertinent to your child's life.

# Owl's World

It had been a busy evening. Piglet and Pooh had learned about the nighttime, and they had met lots of new animals—fireflies, crickets, frogs, mosquitoes, moths, and even an opossum.

Piglet smiled. The next time he met a heffalump, he might just decide to be brave and say "How do you do?" After all, a heffalump might be another interesting creature of the night.

Piglet has trouble falling asleep because, although he tries to be a brave little animal, the truth is that he's afraid of the dark. Certain that the Hundred-Acre Wood is full of heffalumps and other monsters, Piglet visits Pooh for comfort. Pooh suggests consulting Owl, who knows a lot about the nighttime. As Owl takes the two for a walk in the forest, Piglet and Pooh discover that the woods are not full of monsters but of interesting creatures that are active at night. This book will teach children that:

- it's okay to be afraid of the dark.
- it's good to face your fears and conquer them.
- many interesting creatures come out at night.
- it's good to tell someone else about your fears because that person may be able to help you.

## What's It All About?

Children are both intrigued and frightened by the dark. As you ask the following questions about the story, talk about the things — in order — that Owl, Piglet, and Pooh found in the dark. Ask your child whether she thought they were scary or not, and why.

- What did Piglet think was out there in the dark?
- How do crickets make noise?
- How do opossums protect themselves?

- Name the animals that Piglet and Pooh met during their walk in the woods.

## Thinking Time

Before asking the questions below, discuss being afraid with your child. Tell her that everyone is afraid of some things, then ask her to tell you what she is afraid of, and why. Try to come up with creative solutions to dispel her fears. For example, if she's afraid there are monsters under the bed, put a stuffed dinosaur under it and tell her it will "guard" her through the night!

- Why do you think people are afraid of the dark?
- Would you rather be a daytime animal or a nighttime animal?
- Why wasn't Piglet afraid at the end of the story?
- Why do you think Piglet didn't find any heffalumps?

## Moon Walk

Show your child there is nothing to be afraid of at night. Begin with a walk around the child's room, then go from room to room in your house. Open cupboards and peek behind anything that inspires fear in your child.

On your next walk, venture outside, but don't go far. Gradually introducing your child to "night life" will dispel nighttime fears. When you and your child return, discuss what you saw. Do make sure that your child is taught not to go out alone at night, but only with you.

## What Did I See?

Help your child make a list of things that you saw on your night walk that you might not have seen during the daytime. For example: streetlights that are lighted, cars with lights on, insects, stars, the moon.

## A Nighttime Picnic

This is fun to do either with just your child or in a group that might include neighbors with young children. Have your picnic after dark in a tent on the lawn or porch (or in your living room with the lights out), or under a table, or in any setting that will emphasize that it is night. Choose lots of easy-to-eat finger foods and bring along a flashlight or two for making shadow puppets.

## Dark Words

Draw and cut out stars and write words on them with glow-in-the-dark pens. Tape the words to dark spots at night, such as inside closets or behind objects, and have a word hunt. Words you might use are: mosquito, glimpse, butterfly, honeysuckle, peer, firefly, moth, and mouse.